The Neophyte
and
Other Erotic Stories
by
Francesca DiPaolo

Barcelona Press
ISBN #978-0615612027

The Value of Erotica

Sometimes, we all need something to stimulate sexual feelings. Erotica is one way both men and women can create excitement for themselves and their partners, and enjoy a more fulfilling sexual encounter.

These stories were created based on fantasies and real-life experiences told to me by both friends and lovers. Over the years, many have expressed to me their desires, some acted upon and others used only to excite their partners or themselves during the act of love-making. These are shared with you to provide the element of excitement whether you are alone, with a partner, or with multiple partners.

Men have expressed that erotic stories must contain visual elements. Women require that erotica also capture what is in the minds of the characters – descriptions of what they are thinking and feeling. The 10 stories within hopefully capture the elements that will please all readers. Whether for fantasy or re-enactment, I hope you enjoy these tales.

Francesca DiPaolo

CONTENTS

1.
The Neophyte

The woman noticed the girl squatting on the sidewalk as she strode down the street. The girl had her back against the building, a dirty backpack at her side. She didn't seem to be begging but she looked forlorn and unkempt. The hood of her sweatshirt was pulled forward covering her hair, and she looked to be no more than 14 or 15.

Although the woman was in a hurry, she backtracked and stopped in front of the girl. "Are you o.k.?" she asked.

"I'm fine," the girl said glumly. "You don't look fine," said the woman.

For a minute, neither of them spoke. Then the woman said, "You look like you need a hot meal. Why don't you join me for a quick bite," she said as she looked around for a place to eat on the busy Manhattan street. There was a coffee shop at the corner. "We could go over there," she said indicating with a nod toward the coffee shop. The girl didn't move, but she looked like she really wanted the meal. "I don't bite," the woman said with a laugh. "Come on."

The girl got up slowly and the two walked toward the coffee shop. After they were seated, the girl ordered a hamburger and French fries, a soda, side orders of corn and spaghetti and a piece of chocolate cake for dessert. The woman laughed. "Are you sure you can eat all of that?" she asked. The girl nodded but didn't speak.

"So what's your name?" the woman asked. "Kim," the girl answered.

"How old are you Kim?" the woman asked. "I'm 18," said the girl. "Oh, come on," said the woman. "You don't look older than 14."

"Well, I'll be 18 next month," said the girl. "I've always looked younger than I am."

Kim was about 5'4" and weighed no more than 100 lbs. Her build was slender and her breasts were small. She looked under-nourished.

"Where do you live Kim?" the woman asked. "Nowhere in particular," said Kim. "I bunk with friends. Sometimes I stay on the street."

The woman looked concerned. "Where will you sleep tonight?" asked the woman.

"I was looking for a friend who has a place," said the girl, "but I haven't seen him. That's who I was waiting for when you stopped," she said as she bit into the hamburger and stuffed French fries into her mouth.

The woman looked thoughtful for a minute. Then she said, "Look, why don't you come home with me tonight? You'll have to sleep on the couch, but at least you can get a hot shower and you don't have to worry about where you'll sleep today."

The girl looked suspicious. "Look, what do you want from me?" the girl asked.

"What makes you think I want something," asked the woman.

"Everyone wants something," said the girl.

"I'm just offering you a warm place to sleep tonight," said the woman. "No strings attached. It's up to you."

The girl thought for a while. "OK," she said. "But just for tonight."

When they arrived at the apartment, the girl looked around. She walked around the rooms, looking at the photos on the walls, the books on the shelves, the view from the windows. The woman said, "Why don't you let me throw your clothes in the washer. I'll give you a nightgown and you'll have clean clothes in the morning."

The girl took the nightgown and went into the bathroom. She took a long, hot shower and slipped into the woman's long white cotton nightgown. She came out with her dirty clothes in her arms and handed them to the woman. The woman put them in the washer, brought sheets from the closet and made a bed for her on the couch.

The girl stood watching and the woman said, "Why don't you sit down and make yourself comfortable." Once the girl sat on the couch, the woman asked, "Why are you living on the street? Where are your parents?"

At first, the girl was reluctant to answer. But little by little, her story emerged. Her father had died when she was 13 and her mother remarried a man with two sons. Once she and her mother moved into the man's house, the sons began visiting her room at night. At first, they forced her to perform fellatio. They threatened to beat her if she told. Then they began forcing her to have intercourse. When she told her mother, her mother didn't believe her. Her mother then told her stepfather, and he took a strap to her for telling lies about his sons. After a year of abuse, she left home with a girlfriend and had been living on the streets for the last two years.

"But how do you live?" asked the woman. "How do you get money for food?

Before the girl could answer, the front door opened and a man walked in. The girl jumped up. "Who's that?" she asked with a terrified look on her face. "That's just my husband," said the woman. "Don't worry, he won't hurt you."

The man came in and asked, "Who's this?" The woman introduced Kim and explained that she would sleep there for the night. The woman told the girl to relax and she turned on the TV and handed the girl the remote. "Let's go into the kitchen," she said to her husband. As she prepared them a light meal, she told him the story. When they came out of the kitchen, the girl was asleep, the remote still in her hand. "She's perfect," said the husband. "That's what I thought," the woman said and she took the remote, turned off the TV and the lights, and they went to bed.

~ ~ ~

The next morning, the girl was already in her clothes when the woman came to the living room. "I found the washer," the girl said, "and I put my clothes in the dryer. Thanks for everything. I've got to go."

"Wait," said the woman. "I don't have to work today. Why don't you stay for breakfast?"

"OK," said the girl, "but then I've got to go." The man emerged from the bedroom, poured coffee into a travel mug, kissed his wife goodbye and headed out the door.

When the girl had finished her breakfast, the woman suggested they go shopping. "You need a warmer jacket," said the woman. "You can't head into winter with that thin thing," she said.

After some cajoling, the girl agreed and the woman and the girl spent the day shopping, having lunch and going to the movies. For the next several days, the girl continued to sleep on the couch, and the three watched TV, played Scrabble, went to movies and shopped. Then one morning, the woman said to the girl, "We've got to talk."

They sat at the dining room table and the woman said, "You need to think about how you're going to live. This has been fun but you can't stay here like this forever. You don't have a high school diploma, you have no address, no one is going to hire you. I have a way for you to make a lot of money, to have your own apartment, to have a life."

"What do you mean?" asked the girl. "Well, my business is running an escort service," said the woman. "What's that?" asked the girl.

"Well, I provide women to men who are looking for companionship." "You mean, like a date?" asked the girl. "Well, sometimes it's a date," explained the woman, "and sometimes it's more."

"No way," said the girl. "I'm not giving any more blow jobs for $5 or $10."

The woman laughed. "No, not for $5 or $10. You could earn up to $2,500 a night, maybe more if you're good."

The girl's eyes opened wide. "You mean I could make that much just for giving a blow job?" she asked.

The woman laughed again. "No, you'd have to do more than that, but we'd teach you what to do. And men would pay a lot of money for a girl who could pass for 14. You could easily earn us $200,000 a year. Of course, we would take a cut of that, but if we promoted you right, you could make even more."

The girl sat and thought for a while. "What would I have to do?" she asked.

"My husband and I will show you," said the woman. "We'll train you how to satisfy any man's desires. It's not that hard and sometimes it's actually fun. We'll show you how to like it. And even if there are times when you don't, remember how much money you are making and that your life can be anything you want it to be. Are you in?"

"OK," said the girl but she looked worried.

~ ~ ~

That night, the woman took the girl by the hand and led her into the bedroom. The man was already laying on the king sized bed. He was under the sheet and was bare chested. "Come lay between us," said the woman. The girl slid onto the bed and under the sheet. The woman slid in next to her. The woman reached over and helped her out of her nightgown. Her breasts were small and rounded with soft pink nipples just the right size. She had beautiful shoulders and a flat stomach. The man looked her over and said, "You're perfect." The girl blushed.

"Lay down," said the woman, "and face me." The man put his hands on the girl's shoulders and began massaging them and rubbing her back. "Relax," he said.

The woman put her hand on the girl's stomach and said, "I'm going to teach you how to get pleasure first. Then you will be ready to learn how to give pleasure."

The woman put her hand between the girl's legs and began to massage her clitoris. "I want you to focus on the spot I am touching," and as she rubbed the girl's clitoris, it became harder and more pronounced. Then she slid a finger into the girl's vagina and with a come hither motion, moved her finger inside the girl. The girl softly moaned as the man slid his hands down and began to massage her buttocks. The woman lifted the girl's leg onto her hip and the man moved his hips against the girl. He slid his penis between her legs and entered her slowly moving deeper with each thrust.

At the first thrust, the girl gasped and tightened. "Relax," said the woman. "You've done this before." "It's just," said the girl and her voice trailed off as the man moved in and out as the woman continued to massage her clit.

"Focus on my finger," said the woman, "and push down." Suddenly the girl stiffened and her eyes opened wide. "Oh," she moaned loudly and her body shook as she came. "Oh my god," she said. With one last thrust, the man pulled out and came on her back. "We don't want to get you pregnant," he said. That night, the three of them slept side by side, naked and sticky.

~ ~ ~

The next morning over breakfast, the woman told the girl her sex education would continue. "First, we have to get you birth control pills. We'll go to the doctor today. But I want you to learn more about giving pleasure." She went to the TV and inserted a DVD. She and the girl sat together and watched porn videos. Some showed fellatio, and others vaginal sex, anal sex, and three-way sex. The girl was amazed. "I didn't know people did those things," she said.

"Well, men get a lot of pleasure from those things and more," said the woman. "Sometimes they need to watch these to get turned on. I doubt they'll need them with you. But we'll practice more tonight."

13

That night, the three of them lay in bed and the man said, "You need to learn how to give a good blow job."

"I know how to do that," said the girl. "OK, show me," said the man. The girl wrapped her lips around the man's semi-hard penis and began to move up and down. "Not like that," said the man. "Listen to me. It's more about wrapping your tongue around the penis and sucking as you go up. Press your tongue against the bottom of my penis and as you go up, pull the skin down with your hand. And suck it like a lollypop."

As the girl continued, he said, "That's right, you're getting it. Suck it like you love it."

As the woman watched, she reached for a vibrator in the drawer. She rubbed it with lubricant and leaned over the girl. She rubbed the girl's vagina with the oil and them slowly inserted the vibrator into her. And with her other hand, she rubbed the girl's anus and slowly inserted a finger into her ass. The girl flinched and moaned but she kept on sucking the man's dick as the woman massaged her. Suddenly the man moaned loudly and he exploded in the girl's mouth. She started to pull away but the woman pushed her head down and said, "Swallow it."

The cum dripped out of the girl's mouth as she gagged. "You won't be able to do that with clients," she said as she pushed the vibrator deeper into her cunt. Then she removed the vibrator from her cunt and put it against the girl's ass without inserting it.

"Tomorrow," she said, "we'll teach you some new things."

The next night as they lay in bed, the woman explained about anal sex. "This is important to get used to doing and to know how to do it in a way that you don't get hurt."

"Face me," the woman said and she again began massaging the girl's clit. Then she took the vibrator and inserted it into the girl's vagina. The girl quickly became very wet and she moaned softly. The woman put her lips on the girl's and pressed her tongue into the girl's mouth. The girl responded as the man rubbed her from behind. He rubbed lubricant on her ass and slid in a finger. Her ass was tight and could barely accommodate one finger. He moved it in and out and them he inserted a second finger. The girl whimpered but he pressed the fingers fully into her ass. "Focus on my finger," the woman said as she rubbed the girl's clit.

The man removed his fingers and pressed his penis into the girl's ass. "Please don't," she cried. "It hurts." But he held her tightly and pressed into her. "Push out," he said. "Push out as if you were going to the bathroom."

He held her so that she couldn't move and the woman withdrew the vibrator from the girl's cunt. The man thrust into and out of her, pulling his entire penis out and thrusting the head and the shaft in again and again. The girl was sandwiched between the two and couldn't move. "Please stop," she cried.

The man pulled out and the woman said, "I know, it's hard and hurts the first time. But there is no way to make it easy. But it will get easier each time. You'll learn how to bare down and when to relax."

For the next two nights, the couple didn't have sex with the girl. They slept together. They would massage her and touch her but they let her recuperate and get used to the idea. During the days, the woman showed her more porn videos with girl on girl, groups of people, multiple men fucking one woman.

One day, when she and the woman were home alone, both were

15

getting turned on as they watched an anal sex video. "Let's go to the bedroom," said the woman. She reached into the drawer and pulled out two vibrators. They undressed and the woman explained what 69 meant. When they were in that position, the woman said, "Do to me what I do to you."

First, the woman began by sucking the girl's clit and licking her cunt. When the girl was wet, she slid the vibrator into her cunt as she sucked her clit. The woman moaned as the girl sucked her and fucked her. The two of them were so excited that they didn't even hear the man come in. When he saw what was going on, he quickly removed his clothes and lay down behind the girl and entered her ass.

"Oh my god," said the girl and she quickly came. He then moved around to his wife and moved her to the side of the bed. He bent her over the bed and entered her ass with long, hard thrusts. The woman rubbed her clit and then reached for the vibrator and inserted it into her cunt. The man's thrusts became faster and faster until he exploded with cum and as he pulled out, it ran down the woman's legs.

The girl watched in fascination. "I want to try that," she said.

The next night, the woman lay down on the edge of the bed with her legs spread. She told the girl to lick and suck her. The man came up behind the girl and pushed his dick into her ass. "Listen to me," he said. "When I say push, you push and when I say relax, you relax."

"OK," he said as he began to push his dick into her ass. "Push," he said. And as he pulled his penis out, he said "Relax." Soon, the girl was moving in rhythm with the man as she sucked the woman's clit and licked her cunt. Suddenly, the three of them moaned at the same time. Afterwards, they laughed when they realized they had all come simultaneously. "That's a first," said the man.

~ ~ ~

The next day, the woman told the girl that she had a client for her. "You don't know everything you need to know yet," said the woman, "but I have a client who is very eager to meet you. If you please him, he can become a regular and he's good for at least 20 grand a year."

"But I don't know what to do," said the girl. "How do I know what he'll like?"

"Don't worry," said the woman. "He'll show you what he wants and if you act innocent, all the better. He thinks he's getting a 14 year old. You'll just dress like a regular teenager and my husband will take you to him and will wait in the hotel bar. He is paying for two hours and my husband will return to the room to get you. Tonight's the night."

That night, the girl dressed in jeans, a T-shirt, a hoody and sneakers. She and the man took a cab to a hotel, and they took the elevator up to the room. The man knocked on the door and a man about 50 appeared at the door. "Here she is," said the man and he turned and walked away. "Come in," said the john.

"Do you want something to drink?" asked the man. The girl shook her head no. "Take off your sweatshirt," said the man. She took it off and placed it on the chair. "Come here," said the man as he walked toward the bed.

He pulled the girl toward him and unzipped her jeans. He roughly pulled her pants down around her knees, turned her around and bent her over the bed. He pulled his erect penis out of his pants and forced himself into her cunt. At first, she was dry but she quickly became very wet. "Very nice," said the man as he thrust himself again and again into her cunt.

The girl gritted her teeth as the man fucked her. Suddenly, he pulled out and told her to take off her clothes. He removed his pants and told her to lie on her back. He kneeled on the floor and put his tongue into her cunt. "You smell so sweet," said the man. He bent her knees and spread her legs wide. He lay down on her and inserted his penis once again. He fucked her for about ten minutes and then turned her over. This time he reached for lubricant and oiled up her ass.

He pushed his dick against her ass. "Damn, you are tight," he said. She remembered what the couple had taught her, to bare down, then relax, and it became a little easier. The man was heavy and she found it hard to breathe with his weight on her. Suddenly, he pulled out and came on her back. He collapsed next to her and lay there for while.

After a few minutes, he told her to go to the bathroom and wash off. When she returned, he was playing with himself and was hard once again. "Let me look at you," he said. "Lay down here." He licked her breasts and her stomach, then sucked her cunt and then her asshole. He made grunting sounds as he put his fingers in her cunt, then in his mouth, sucking off her cunt juice. The he said, "Suck my dick."

She bent over him and gave a blow job the way the man had showed her. The john moaned as she sucked him and she took his dick deep into her throat without gagging. She had become very practiced at fellatio. Finally, the man came and he seemed to lose interest in her. She went to the bathroom and rinsed her mouth. She put on her clothes and waited to be picked up. She didn't realize the man had paid $2,500 for what he thought was a 14 year old. It would just be one of many such jobs to come, the beginning of what would be a fortune in the course of a few years.

2.
The Cougar

He was 25 and the woman he was about to meet was almost twice his age. He met her on a "cougar" dating site, a place where younger men hooked up with older women. They had communicated for a while and it took many messages for him to convince her he was not too young.

He had a long held fantasy about having sex with an older woman. To him, they seemed more at peace with themselves and comfortable with their sexuality. He was tired of women his own age who were drama queens, girls who easily became jealous, wanted his complete attention and kept pressuring for a more committed relationship. An older woman, he thought, who had her own life and who only wanted pleasure and companionship was more to his liking.

He stood in front of her door and gathered his courage before he rang the bell. Even though he was the initiator, he was nervous. He took a deep breath and pressed the buzzer. After a few moments, he heard footsteps and then the door opened. He was relieved that she looked exactly like her photo. She smiled at him and said, "Come on in."

She led him into the kitchen. "Would you like a glass of wine?" she asked. "That would be nice," he said. She poured two glasses and led him to the living room. She sat down on the couch and motioned for him to sit next to her. They made small talk until she finally said, "I can't keep up this conversation. All I can think about is what I know we both want to do."

He leaned toward her and kissed her. He instantly felt his semi-hard dick become hard and press uncomfortably against his pants. He reached for her hand and placed it on his dick. "Oh my god," she moaned. "Let's go where we can be more comfortable."

She took his hand and led him to her bedroom. He began to take off his clothes and she said, "Let me do it."

She unbuttoned his cotton shirt and kissed his chest. His chest had light fuzz but was not overly hairy. She inhaled his scent and said, "You smell good." She slipped off his shirt and struggled to unbutton his jeans. He helped her take them off. He kissed her deeply, sucking her tongue and pressing his tongue into her mouth. She tasted fresh and her mouth was appealing. He thought how good his dick would feel in it.

She began to slide down his boxers and she dropped to her knees and took his dick into her mouth as his underwear dropped around his ankles. Her mouth felt like fire as she sucked his dick, her tongue wrapped tightly around the underside of his penis, the head of his dick against the back of her throat. When she pulled her mouth back, her hand gently pulled the skin of his penis away from her mouth, and she repeated this each time she took him in.

After a few minutes, she stood up and whispered in his ear, "Lay down." He stepped out of his underwear and lay down on the bed. His dick was rock hard and stood straight in the air.

She slipped out of her clothes and unbuttoned her bra. Her breasts were small but full and she had amazing nipples. She removed her panties and he was surprised to see she had hair around her pussy. Most of the young women he dated had removed all their hair. He found her fluff very erotic.

She knelt over him and spread the lips of her cunt apart and lowered herself onto his dick. Her cunt was wet and hot and, as she rocked back and forth, she reached out for his hands so she could better balance and rise up and down on his dick.

No cunt had never felt this good to him before. The heat and texture of her pussy were amazing and he said, "That's it. Fuck me hard. Come on, do it, do it." He watched as her tits bounced with every move she made.

She was moaning and so wet that his body became wet with her juices. Just then, she pulled off of him and began to suck his dick, licking off her cunt juice. Then she began to lick and suck his balls. She reached for a pillow and slipped it under his ass so she could better reach his asshole. At first, she tentatively passed her tongue over his anus to test his reaction. He reached down and began to stroke his dick.

She spread his butt cheeks with her hands and plunged her tongue into his anus as far as it would go. His ass was smooth and clean tasting. She reached for a tube of lubricant on the night table, oiled his anus and gently inserted one narrow finger, a little at first, and then deeply. As she did this, she began sucking his dick, alternating the rhythm with her finger and her mouth. He moaned softly and concentrated on not coming.

Suddenly he sat up and flipped her onto her back. He spread her legs apart and admired her cunt. It was purplish red and her lips were wide open. The labia were wet and shiny and he buried his head between her legs and began licking her. He sucked her hard clit and inserted a finger into her cunt. He pushed his finger in and out roughly and she said, "No, slow down and just rub the back."

He followed her direction and she began moving her hips to the rhythm of his finger.

"In my ass," she said. "He licked his finger and inserted it into her ass, keeping the other hand in her cunt with one, then two fingers the way she liked it. He continued sucking her clit.

She reached down and pushed his mouth away and began masturbating, rubbing her clit hard and fast as he continued to finger her cunt and her ass. Suddenly, she began to moan and her body stiffened. "Oh my god, oh my god," she said and let out a long, primal cry. It seemed to go on forever, but after a few minutes she quieted but continued to breath deeply.

He lifted himself onto her and began fucking her in the missionary position. She wrapped her legs around him and rocked with the motion as they kissed and sucked one another's tongues.

Suddenly he pulled out and pulled her over to the side of the bed. "What are you doing?" she asked. "Just bend over," he said as he pressed her down onto the bed with her ass in the air. He began fucking her from behind. When he noticed the lube on the night table, he grabbed it and oiled her ass. He spread her cheeks and pressed the bright red head of his dick into her ass. She moaned as he pushed the head in and then pulled it out. "You're too big," she said. "You're hurting me."

"Hold on," he said as he pulled out his dick and he poured the lube right into her ass. He then put his dick up to her anus but he didn't push. "Relax," he said. He rested his dick against her ass hole and slid it in by millimeters. Suddenly he pushed hard until his entire dick was in as she cried out in pain. He couldn't believe how tight she felt. "Oh shit," he said. "You feel so good." "Fuck me, fuck me," she said and he went wild, pounding her until he came and they both collapsed on the bed.

They lay there together for a while before either of them spoke. "You felt really good," he said. "I love the way your cunt feels and tastes," he said as he slid a finger into her soaking wet cunt.

He liked having the freedom to touch her wherever he felt without having her push him away as other women had done. He leaned over and sucked on her big nipples. "I can't get enough of you," he said. "Mmm," she responded and they both fell asleep.

~ ~ ~

She was still asleep in the morning when he woke up. He was surprised that he had allowed himself to fall asleep and stay the night, something he would not normally do. It took him a few seconds to realize he was lying in bed next to this woman. Her back was toward him and he pressed his already hard morning dick against her behind. He reached around her and cupped her breast. She moaned softly and she repositioned herself so he could fuck her cunt. He slid his dick in and they moved slowly for a few minutes. Then he pulled out and turned her around, kissing her gently, rubbing her stomach, her buttocks, her thighs. "I want to touch every inch of your body," he said.

He turned around so he was in the right position for 69. He began sucking her clit, then inserting his tongue into her cunt while she sucked his dick with her amazing mouth. "Wait," she said and she rolled over to the night table drawer. She reached in and pulled out a vibrator that had an undulating shape – narrow, then wider, narrow and wider again. She lubed the vibrator and turned it on.

"Put this in my ass," she said. "Push it in the whole way and then pull it out completely a few times then just hold it in deep."

They went back to 69 and he did as she asked. He pushed the vibrator in, watching her ass open with the wide part and then close again around the narrow part. He felt extremely turned on watching this and repeated it three times. Then he pushed it the entire way in with just an inch or so outside. He held it hard into her ass while he licked her cunt and sucked her clit.

At the same time, she was sucking on him hard, forcing his dick as deep into her throat as she could. Suddenly, she erupted with a moan so deep and long that it scared him. But at the same time, he exploded into her throat and she held onto his dick so that she captured all of his cum.

They lay like that for a while and finally, he lay facing her and said, "You are unbelievable. I've never had sex this intense before."

"You're not bad yourself," she said. "We should do this again," he said. "Often."

She smiled. "We'll see," she said. And with that, she got up and handed him his clothes. "I think you should go now," she said. "I'll call you."

He dressed and she walked him to the door. She kissed him and said, "That was wonderful. Thank you."

He hugged her and kissed her lightly on the lips. "Until next time," he said and he walked to his car smiling.

3.
The Three-Way

From the beginning, he told her he wanted to explore sexually. While their sex had been energetic and exploratory, he wanted to push the limits. "I want to look into your eyes while someone else is fucking you," he said.

She was comfortable with him and felt she could trust him, and although his fantasies were enticing, she was apprehensive about the reality. "I'll just plan it and surprise you," he told her, "so you won't have to worry about it beforehand."

"Is there something you want to do with another man," she asked. "No, I just want to watch you," he said, but she wasn't sure about his intentions.

One night at his apartment, he led her into the bedroom and undressed her. He loved to take off her clothes and slip off her underwear. There was something very titillating about removing her lingerie – silky, skimpy things she wore just to please him.

He kissed her lips and lay her down on the bed. He sucked her ample nipples and slid down to lick her already juicy cunt. He spread her legs and lifted them in the air to get better access to her pussy and to her ass. He loved the color of her cunt, a raw purplish color, glossy and ripe looking. He lifted her ass and pressed his tongue deep into it. He loved the way her ass tasted and she moaned as he inserted his tongue as far as it would go.

He flipped her onto her stomach and positioned her so that her head was at the foot of the bed. He put a pillow under her hips, raising her ass slightly so he could put his penis into her cunt. She purred at the sensation.

He reached for a bottle of lube and poured some on her asshole. He then spread her butt cheeks and inserted a dildo into her ass. It was wider at the head than in the shaft and she grunted a little, but she didn't resist as he slid it deep into her ass.

Suddenly, the door to the bedroom opened and a man walked in. She lifted her head in alarm and said, "Who the hell are you."

"He's your gift honey," said her lover. "Just relax and enjoy."

The man knelt down and kissed her, gently at first, and then inserted his tongue into her mouth. At first she was apprehensive, but she quickly responded to him as her lover moved in her cunt and pressed the dildo into her ass. The man stood up and unzipped his pants. A long, thick penis popped out. She smiled in appreciation. He pushed his hard dick into her mouth and she sucked it greedily.

Her lover became even more aroused and he moved more rapidly in and out of her. She moaned with pleasure as she lifted and lowered her hips to take in as much of his dick as she could.

Suddenly, her lover removed the dildo and pulled out of her. He motioned for the man to pull back. He turned the woman over and told her to stand at the foot of the bed, facing him. He knelt on the bed facing her and began kissing her. The second man bent her over slightly and began fucking her cunt.

Her lover looked her in the eyes and said, "That's it. Take it, take that big dick."

Now she was moaning as she felt the second man's dick in her cunt and his hands on her ass, moving her to his rhythm. Her lover alternated between sucking her nipples and looking her in the eyes saying, "Take it baby. Take that big dick. Fuck him."

The second man then pressed his dick into her ass. "Ow," she whimpered and tried to pull away. "Come on baby," said her lover. "Take it in your ass. You know you like it."

Now the second man was pounding her. He was holding her by the hips so she could not slip away. Her lover then stood on the bed so that his dick was near her face. He began jerking off as he watched her being fucked. "Open your mouth," he said.

He grabbed her by the face and forced her mouth open. Big huge squirts of cum shot into her mouth. Just then, the second man withdrew his dick from her ass and came on her backside. The three of them then collapsed on the bed.

They lay there side by side, the woman in the middle, sticky and wet. "Did you like that?" asked her lover. "You might have warned me," she said. She turned to the other man. "At least you can tell me your name." "Hi, I'm Peter," he said and the three of them laughed.

"And where did he find you Peter?" she asked. Her lover told her he went to AdultFriendFinder.com and looked for someone who wanted to have sex with a couple. "There were lots of options," he said. "Did I choose well?" "I'll say you did," as she smiled at the tall, good-looking man with the athletic build. Although her lover had a nice body, this man was even more appealing.

Her lover left the room and came back with a bottle of wine and three glasses. They chatted about their sexual experiences and the more they talked, the more the three of them became turned on again. She turned to face Peter and began kissing him and caressing his dick. Her lover reached between her legs and fingered her cunt.

Peter then lifted her onto her lover so that her lover's dick could enter her ass from behind. Peter reached for the lube and poured some on his hand and rubbed it onto her lover's dick. She couldn't see what was happening but if she did, she would have been surprised that her lover did not react badly. In fact, he moved in rhythm to the man's hand. The man directed the dick into her ass and then positioned himself so he could fuck her cunt.

Now they were both in her and she moaned as they moved in and out of her. Her lover could feel the other man's balls touching his and it excited him in a way that he had never experienced before.

Suddenly, the woman began to moan loudly and cry out. At the sound of her cries, her lover exploded in her ass and slid out. Peter continued to pound her and she wrapped her legs around him until he came.

They lay in a heap, legs entangled, sticking to one another. No one said anything. No one knew what to say. The three of them drifted into sleep. They had been at it for hours.

A few hours later, the woman awoke to find Peter sucking her lover's dick. She watched in amazement. Her lover had always denied wanting to do anything with a man, but now he lay there with a look on his face she had never seen before. He turned to look at her and reached over to touch her. She reached over and kissed him passionately.

Peter then let go of her lover's dick and lifted his legs in the air. She stopped kissing him and watched as Peter pressed his dick into her lover's ass. The site of this turned her on so much that she reached for the dildo and began to masturbate, moving the dildo in and out as she massaged her clit. She never imagined she could be ready again this soon, but lying next to her lover, watching him get fucked was more erotic than she could have imagined.

With the dildo still inside her, she leaned over and took her lover's dick in her mouth. As Peter moved in and out of him, she sucked her lover's dick until he came in her mouth. Once he came, Peter let go and came in her lover's ass.

Once he withdrew his dick from her lover, he sat on the edge of the bed for a few minutes. Without looking at them, he said, "I have to go." He put on his clothes and left the room. They heard the front door close and they lay there in silence.

4.
The Strap On

Their love making had been energetic and creative. They satisfied one another in all the usual ways. He loved to lick her shiny, purple cunt and suck her large clit. She loved to suck his 7-inch dick and especially liked to take it in all the way to the back of her throat while she stroked the base of his penis. He sucked her large, pink nipples and she sucked his. They kissed passionately while she sat on his dick, clamping down on him with her cunt, tightening and loosening until he groaned with pleasure.

They both enjoyed anal activity. Early on, he had fucked her ass until she begged him to stop. She loved licking his anus, then inserting a finger while she sucked his dick. One night he surprised her by sucking her anus and pressing his tongue into her as far as it would go. She moaned with the pleasure of this new experience.

They became very open and comfortable with one another as their relationship progressed. One night, she showed him her collection of vibrators and dildos and he admired them with wonder. He took each of them and inserted them into her to see how far they would go. He placed a large one with protruding bumps into her vagina and gently rotated it. She had already come so she didn't find it arousing, but she was amused as she watched him play with the toys.

He lubed up a smaller vibrating one and eased it into her ass as he rubbed her clit with his thumb. He looked completely fascinated. He removed it and eased one with an undulating shape into her ass and another into her cunt. He turned on the vibration and she began to moan. She was turned on again. He leaned down and began to suck her clit and then he lay on top of her, sucking her tongue as he continued to maneuver the vibrators in her ass and cunt. To her amazement, she came again, moaning and crying loudly. He had never heard her make that sound before.

"Take them out, please," she asked after she had come. He kneeled in front of her, removed the vibrator from her cunt and placed it in his mouth. "Delicious," he said. Then he eased the larger one from her ass.

"Do you want to try one," she asked. "Not tonight," he said. "Maybe another time." He lay down on his back and began stroking his dick. "Come and do me with your hand," he said.

She reached for the lube and rubbed it over his dick and began stroking him. "Go all the way up and over the head," he instructed her and she did as he asked. He loved the way she masturbated him. While his own hand gave him the result he wanted, it was never as good as when she did it.

She loved watching him this way. And he loved watching her stroke his dick. They continued on for a while and suddenly he said, "It's coming." Huge squirts of white cum shot out of his dick, slowing and then shooting out some more. She had never seen so much cum in one ejaculation. When he stopped, she rubbed it over his stomach, on his dick and balls. Then she leaned down and sucked his shrunken dick. "That feels so good," he said.

She got up and got a warm washcloth and cleaned him off. She lay next to him and stroked the hair on his chest. "I love this body," she said as she kissed his chest and inhaled his smell. She loved his aroma, the texture of his skin, the fact that his tall, lean physique overpowered her small frame. She loved being fucked by him.

~ ~ ~

Following this session, their e-mail messages became more erotic. They teased each other about things they wanted to do to one another. In one, he indicated that he wanted to add a strap on to her collection. She wasn't sure about his intent, whether he wanted it in his ass, or for double penetration in hers. Either way, she was fine with it. "You buy it," she told him, "And I'll wear it."

Early on, he had been sensitive about his ass. The first time she licked him there, she asked if he liked it. "It was interesting," he said. She didn't know whether that was good or indifferent or if he had never experienced it before, although that was hard to imagine as he seemed very experienced sexually. During a following session, she tried to put a finger in his anus and he said, "Not too far in."

She knew that men were sensitive about admitting that they enjoyed anal penetration because such an admission might imply that they had homosexual desires. She knew instinctively that this was not the case as she well understood the sexual arousal from anal penetration.

The next time they met, he arrived with a bag. "What's that?" she asked. "It's for you," he said. She looked in the bag and discovered a strap-on dildo, not too long, perhaps about 7 inches. "Well," she said, "we'll have to experiment."

This night, after enjoying deep, passionate kisses and mutual masturbation, they shifted into position for 69. She lubed her index finger and as she sucked his dick, she inserted a finger into his anus. She moved it in and out as she licked his dick, sucking just the engorged head, and then sliding her mouth almost down to the base.

In the meantime, he had her legs spread and fingered her engorged cunt as he sucked her clit. They were both on the verge of coming when he pulled back and said, "Fuck me."

"What," she asked. She wasn't sure if she had heard him correctly. "Fuck me," he said, "with this." He reached for the strap on. She shifted herself around and slipped it on, adjusting the straps so it fit her body. She couldn't believe she had this dick sticking out of her, something she had always fantasized about. She was even more turned on.

He lay on his back facing her. He put a pillow under his ass and lifted his legs. He rubbed lube on his ass and said, "Go easy."

She put the rounded head of it up to his ass but it was too big to go in. She rubbed lube on her fingers and slid one into his ass, then a second, and then a third. Her fingers were small and it took three fingers to open him up.

She pulled out her fingers and placed the head of the dildo up against his ass, much in the way she had seen men do to women in porn movies. She pressed the head in slightly and then pulled it out. She repeated this a few times until the head was finally into his ass. She leaned into the dildo until the entire thing was in him. Now her body was up against his, and she rocked back and forth watching the dildo slide in and out.

He watched her as she did this. His dick was hard and he was stroking it. They kept at this for a while when he suddenly said, "Take it off." She pulled out and removed the device. He flipped her around and bent her over doggie style. He slid his dick into her cunt, pounding her as her cunt juice ran down over his dick and onto the bed. Suddenly, they exploded and moaned simultaneously. He held his dick in her as long as he could until it slipped out and they collapsed onto a huge wet spot on the bed.

"We've been fucked," she said. And they both began to laugh as they inhaled the deep, rich smell of sex that surrounded them.

5.

Two Cocks

They sat on the couch talking, occasionally kissing. She touched him affectionately, caressing his shaved head, kissing his neck, inhaling his scent. She was pouring him another glass of wine when the doorbell rang. "Finally," she said.

She went to the door and kissed a tall, well-built handsome man with a goatee. "Peter, I'm glad you could come," she said and she led him into the living room. She introduced him to the Roger, a rugged looking man with caramel colored skin.

She was petite and buxom with long blond hair pulled to the back of her head with a clip. She wore a filmy white shirt over a floor length cotton print skirt. Her breasts jiggled beneath her blouse without the restriction of a bra.

The two men sat across from one another and began chatting about a recent game where the favored team lost badly. She poured them both more wine and sat down next to Peter. She casually placed her hand on his crotch and began stroking him. He interrupted his conversation and leaned over to kiss her. She put her tongue deep into his mouth and continued to rub his dick. Finally, she unzipped his pants and pulled out his already hard penis and began masturbating him.

Roger unzipped his pants and pulled out his penis as he watched the woman jerking off the man. Suddenly, she knelt on the floor in front of Peter and began sucking his dick. He reached into her blouse and caressed her breast. It was soft and full and he thought he would come just at the feel of it, but he steeled himself to prolong the pleasure.

Roger approached her as she knelt and pulled her up so her ass was in the air. He lifted her skirt and was delighted to see she had no underwear. Her ass was silky white and he put his dick, which was darker than the rest of his body, next to her ass. The contrast excited him and he touched her cunt to make sure she was wet.

When he removed his hand, it was covered with the shiny juice of her cunt. "Jesus," he said. He pressed his dick into her cunt and pushed it all the way in. She moaned deeply as she continued to suck Peter's dick. She pushed her ass toward Roger and he moved his dick in and out slowly but with deep penetration.

The woman stood up and Roger's dick slid out as she rose. She lifted her blouse over her head and removed it. She turned around and kissed Roger deeply. She lifted her skirt and lowered herself onto Peter's dick placing her just at the right height to put Roger's dick in her mouth.

After a few minutes, she said, "It's not comfortable here. Let's go upstairs." She led the way in only her skirt and the two men followed. When they got to the bedroom, the men removed their shoes and their clothes. She took off her skirt and lay down on the bed, and said, "Who wants me?" Roger knelt on the bed and began sucking her shiny, wet pussy. She was shaved and her cunt looked like a little girl's except that her clit was hard and extended, and looked like a tiny penis. He sucked it hard and she draped her legs over his shoulders. She motioned for Peter to come closer to her head. He lay next to her with his dick close to her face and she began sucking it wildly as

Roger reached for the lube on the bedside table and oiled her ass. He raised her legs in the air and his cock was positioned to enter her ass. He pressed into her and she cried from the pain. Peter bent down to quiet her cries with a kiss as Roger pressed deep into her ass and began moving in a steady rhythm. "You're hurting me," she said, but Roger did not stop. Peter sucked her breasts and watched her face as Roger went in and out as deeply as his cock would go. Suddenly, he pulled out and said, "I don't want to come yet."

Peter rolled the woman over and placed her on her knees with her ass in the air and her head on the bed. He spread her cheeks and saw that her ass was wide open. He reached for the lube and poured some down the crack of her ass. Then he slid his dick in and groaned, "Oh my god. I don't believe how tight you feel," and he pounded her hard, again and again, until she pleaded with him to stop. He pulled out and began licking and sucking her ass. Roger masturbated as he watched what Peter was doing.

"I think you need a break," Peter said, and he lay down next to her, caressing her ample breasts. "You have great nipples," he told her as he licked the round, soft brown orb of her left breast. Roger lay on the other side of her and placed one finger, than two inside her cunt. He removed his fingers, licked them and inserted them again. Then he extended his hand over to Peter and said, "Lick it." The second man opened his mouth and sucked the cunt juice off the first man's fingers.

"You both think it's great to be rough with my ass," she said, "but I'd like to see if you could take it." "Is that a challenge?" asked Peter. "Yes," she said. "Let me give it to you in the ass."

"How are you going to that?" he asked. And with that, she reached into the night table drawer and pulled out a slim, straight vibrator and a glass dildo that looked like a series of balls connected together.

"With these," she said. She knelt over him and poured lube on her hand. She rubbed some on his asshole and the rest on her fingers. She lifted his legs in the air, and slipped a finger into his ass. As she did this, she put his dick in her mouth and sucked him slowly sliding her mouth up and down.

After he took a finger for a few minutes, she slipped the narrow vibrator into his asshole. "Easy," he said, but he did not complain as she slowly slid it in and out, a little deeper with each stroke. Roger stroked his cock as he watched the action. Suddenly, he moved the woman out of the way and removed the vibrator from Peter's ass. He pressed his dick into Peter's ass and after a few strokes, Peter came with cum shooting up on his chest. He moaned as Roger continued to pound his ass.

Roger pulled out and the woman said, "Now it's your turn." She made him kneel with his ass up and she lubed the knobbed dildo. First she licked his ass and then inserted a finger into his asshole. Then, as she reached under him to stroke his dick, she slowly inserted the dildo into his ass. Peter now sat up and watched with curiosity as the dildo widened Roger's asshole and then closed as it reached the narrow portion of the dildo. Peter grabbed the vibrator and reached around the woman and slid the vibrator into her ass. He pushed the button to start the vibration and he moved it slowly in and out of her asshole.

Suddenly, Roger came with a loud moan. The woman then reached around to stroke her clit as Peter continued to fuck her ass with the vibrator. She let out a cry and a long whimper and finally a deep moan. She lay down next to Roger and Peter lay on the other side of her. The three of them lay panting next to one another. Finally, the woman said, "We have to do this again sometime," and the two men agreed. "How about in another hour," said Peter and the three of them laughed.

6.

The Hookup

They flirted online for weeks and they finally agreed to meet in Manhattan for lunch in two weeks time. But during the two weeks, the flirting turned sexual and he asked her if he should book a room or if she would like to go to his place. She demurred thinking she didn't want to back herself into a corner. What if she didn't like him when she met him? Finally she said, let's play it by ear. But as the date got closer and their conversation got hotter, she e-mailed him the message: Why don't you book a room?

He was skeptical. Would she really show up? Was he being played or set up? But he finally decided to take a chance. He had enough points to get a room for free so he figured he did not have too much to lose. Besides, it had been months since he had gotten laid and this woman interested him. She was bright and funny and had the kind of slim body and small proportions he liked.

She was surprised at her own response. She hadn't done anything like this before and wasn't sure why she was doing it now. Maybe after years of following the rules, she was ready for adventure. But there was something about him, an expression he had in his photo and the way he expressed himself in his e-mail that drew her to him.

She arrived in the lobby of the hotel 20 minutes early and found a seat on a couch where she could see him approach. She took off her coat and began checking e-mail on her iPhone. She became so engrossed in her messages that she didn't see him approach. He sat down in the chair next to her, smiled and said, "Hi."

She looked up and smiled. "Well, look at you," she said. "You're adorable." He grinned and she was charmed by his smile. They had agreed before meeting that a hug would be appropriate to break the ice. As they did, she noted how good he smelled.

They chatted about who knows what, and then he moved next to her on the couch and touched her hand and her leg in a way that someone might assume they were already familiar. They agreed to have lunch and set off to find a place to eat.

Once they settled in at the table, he told her he was writing a book about his life. Sure, she thought, you and everybody else. But once he began regaling her with stories about his life, she realized he really was on to something and they began to imagine a movie version.

By the time they got to the room, she was totally charmed. He was not only hot, but he was interesting and sweet, which made what was about to happen even more enticing. They kissed and it was electric. They began taking off their clothes and when he unzipped his pants, his dick popped out. It was long and thick. She made a slight gasping noise and said, "That's a pleasant surprise."

She knelt on the bed and he said, "Why is your underwear still on?" "I want you to take them off," she said. When he removed her bra, he said, "Look at those nipples!" They were extended and her small, white breasts made them look even larger. He began sucking one and then the other. Then, he lay her down on the bed and spread her legs. He was amazed by the size of her clit and how plump and shiny it was. He began sucking it and she moaned as he alternated sucking it and inserting his tongue into her cunt.

Suddenly, he lifted himself up and positioned himself to fuck her. She helped guide his penis into her cunt, and he kissed her. "You taste like cunt," she said and smiled. "I like it." He liked the way this woman was so open and natural about sex, and he found himself feeling comfortable and open for anything.

He began to move inside her and she lifted herself up to take all of him in. She had never particularly liked the missionary position but he filled her up in a way that was so satisfying that she couldn't believe it. They moved like this for a long time and when they kissed, they alternated sucking one another's tongues and lips.

He didn't want to come just yet, so he moved off of her, kissing her and taking her into his arms. They talked and soon were kissing and touching one another again. She kissed his chest and slowly moved down to his cock and sucked it. She licked it from the tip to the base and then sucked the head. Slowly, she took him in as far as the back of her throat, enjoying the feeling of him filling her up. He moaned softly.

When he could take it no more, he flipped her over and positioned her on her knees. He entered her from behind. He held her by the hips as he roughly pounded her cunt. "Who's my bitch?" he said as he slapped her on the ass. "I am," she said. "I'm your whore, this cunt is yours," and he slapped her again.

She moaned with pleasure. She had never been this excited.

"Harder," she said and he slapped her harder. She was shocked by the sudden eruption of an orgasm, one more intense than she had ever experienced before. She moaned loudly and whimpered. He pulled out of her and gathered her in his arms. They lay there breathing heavily and soon decided they were hungry. Checking the room service menu, they ordered lava cake and laughed at the irony of it.

They ate the cake naked in bed. Then they lay together and talked as she stroked his dick. He put his finger in her cunt and then sucked off her juices. They laughed and he quickly became hard again. She slipped her head down and began sucking his cock. But this time, she licked his balls and ran her tongue over his asshole. Then she licked her finger and pressed it gently into his asshole as she returned to sucking his dick. Since he didn't object, she slid her finger all the way into his ass. "I've never had it so deep before," he said. He felt as if he was ready to come but he wasn't ready. He wanted more. He pulled her up and put his dick in her cunt as she sat astride him.

This time, he not only filled her up, he pressed at the back of her vagina. She moaned and thought she would come again, but she held herself back, wanting to extend the pleasure. She leaned over and kissed him and then whispered in his ear, "I also like it in my ass." He smiled and said, "I'd like putting it in your ass."

She reached for the lube she had brought and rubbed it on his cock. He bent her over the edge of the bed and lubed her asshole. He pressed his dick into her. She had never taken anything so large and it hurt. She whimpered as he pressed into her. "Do you want me to stop?" he asked. "No," she said, "keep going. Oh my god, it hurts," she said.

"Then you push," he told her and she pushed in slow increments until the pain subsided a bit, and then she pushed some more. When he was completely in, it was so tight there almost wasn't room for movement. When he tried to slide out or in, it felt to her that his cock was stuck. He smacked her ass and reached over and cupped her breasts in his hands. She moaned at both the pain and the pleasure. He pulled out and turned her around, lifted her up so her legs were around his waist. He kissed her as he inserted his dick into her cunt and held her tight to him. He lay her down on the bed and began sucking her cunt and inserted a finger into her asshole. She moved her hips to give him better access.

He lifted her ass up and looked at her asshole. It was pink and open from his dick. He began licking her, inserting his tongue as far as it would go. She couldn't believe the intensity of the feeling. Suddenly, he inserted his finger into her ass and removed it, sitting up and sucking his finger. "You're disgusting," she said. "I know," he responded and they both laughed.

He entered her again missionary style and she wrapped her legs around him, rocking with his rhythm until she exploded with another intense orgasm. After she came, he pulled out and stood over her on the bed. He stoked his penis twice and then exploded on her stomach and chest in great spurts of cum. Then he lay on top of her and entered her again for a few more strokes, pulled out and continued coming.

They smiled at one another and he lay down on top of her with the cum gluing their bodies together. They smiled as they looked into one another's eyes and finally fell asleep.

7.
The Masturbator

She had been watching him masturbate on a sex dating site for months. Every few weeks, he would post a new video, sometimes jerking off with his hand, other times with a toy that simulated a vagina. His dick was large and beautiful, she thought, with an engorged, angled head at the end of a thick 8 inches or so that looked like it could provide a lot of pleasure.

She didn't think of herself as a voyeur, although she was becoming obsessed with watching him. Although she sometimes viewed porn videos followed by a session with a vibrator, watching men masturbate was what turned her on the most.

As the Masturbator approached orgasm, his breathing would become heavier and when he began to come, he would grunt ever so slightly and the cum would shoot out in great, powerful spurts. Even after he came, his dick remained erect.

Sometimes during sex, she would imagine herself having a dick. As her partner fingered her cunt and as she stroked his dick, she liked to transpose the feeling inside her to the dick, as if it was hers. This erotic thought would sometimes make her come, even before her partner entered her.

She had always been fascinated with penises. She loved looking at them and had a collection of books with photos of all shapes and sizes. As much as she loved looking at them, she loved handling them. But most of all, she loved sucking them. Well, most of them.

She had quickly jettisoned men whose dicks were too small, too hairy, too misshapen. She was amazed at the variety she encountered and often stayed with men longer than she should have because their dicks were so spectacular.

But she kept returning to the masturbator. One day, she was so aroused that she sent him a message. "I love to watch you come," she wrote. "I have been watching you for months and I would love to suck that dick and then sit on it."

She couldn't believe that she wrote something that graphic, but with the safety she felt behind the keyboard, she let herself go. She didn't begin to think about what she would do if he responded to her. In fact, it never occurred to her that he would. But a few days later, a message popped up saying, "I would like to watch you come too."

The thought of recording her private parts was repugnant to her and she didn't feel it was something she could do. She was not confident enough about her body to display it to the world, only to one man at a time in a dimly lit room.

She wrote back, "I'd rather show you in person." She assumed that the Masturbator was just another exhibitionist who got pleasure from jerking off in front of the camera. She didn't expect that he would be brave enough to accept her challenge. In fact, she wasn't sure that she was brave enough. But his response came in a few minutes.

"Send me your photo," he responded. "Here's mine." He was tall and muscular and rather nice looking. If she had seen him on the street, she would have never imagined that he masturbated in front of a camera and posted it on the internet.

She sent a photo of herself clothed, but enticing. When he didn't respond right away, she assumed he didn't like what he saw. She was disappointed and a little hurt, but the next day, a message from him appeared. "I would like to meet you," he wrote. "Let's see how we get along and we'll take it from there."

They arranged to meet at a local coffee house at 2:00 in the afternoon. She got there early so she wouldn't have to walk in and look for him. Let him be the one like a deer in the headlights, she thought.

At 2:00 on the dot, he walked in and looked exactly like his photo. He smiled at her from the entrance and walked over to the table. He put out his hand and said, "Nice to meet you."

They ordered coffee and made small talk. Where do you live, what do you do, where have you traveled? When they ran out of conversation, he said, "So why do you like to watch me jerk off?"

She blushed. "I like your cock," she said. "It's big and voluptuous and every time I would watch you, I'd want to put my mouth around it."

He stirred in the chair as if to shift his dick and balls. He smiled. "That's the idea," he said.

"But why do you like to do it online," she asked. "I don't really know," he said, "but it turns me on to think someone is watching. And besides, you liked it and if I hadn't done it, you wouldn't be here right now, would you?"

"I always wanted to have a dick," she said laughing. "I think I suffer from penis envy."

They both laughed and he said, "I like you. So where do we go from here?"

"I feel as if I need to get to know you a little better before we get physical," she said, but in reality, she was already wet thinking about what it would be like to fuck him.

"Why don't you come to my house for dinner tomorrow," he suggested. "We don't have to do anything unless it feels right for you. Let's just have dinner and talk and we can see where it goes. I won't be upset if you don't want to do anything yet. As a matter of fact, if we hold off for a while, it will be even better when it happens."

She agreed and they left. On the sidewalk, he leaned toward her and firmly pulled her toward him. But he surprised her by landing the gentlest of kisses on her lips. He pulled away and looked at her and he said, "Until tomorrow," and he turned and walked down the street.

~ ~ ~

The next day when she told her friends about the episode, they were appalled that she would agree to go to the house of a man she hardly knew. They warned her about every possible gruesome scenario, but she could not be convinced. She was obsessed with his dick and was compelled to have sex with him. She dropped the subject and told her friends she would not go.

But at 7:00 p.m., she arrived at the address he gave her. When he opened the door, he looked great, she thought. A casual cotton button front shirt hung over a pair of jeans. He kissed her lightly on the cheek and he smelled freshly showered. "Come on in," he said.

The aroma of good cooking filled the air. He poured her a glass of wine and motioned for her to follow him to the kitchen. They chatted about food, their lives and other details. After dinner, they sat in front of a smoldering fire in the fireplace. He leaned over and kissed her gently and slid his hand between her thighs. She was immediately aroused and put her hand on his erect dick. He unzipped his pants and his dick came out. She realized that he was not wearing any underwear.

He eased her down to the floor in front of the fire and lifted her skirt. She had only a thong underneath, and he moved it aside as he licked her cunt. She was already wet and he slid the tip of his tongue up and down the length of her labia, stopping at her clit to suck it and then sliding his tongue the length of it again. He lifted her butt and began to lick her anus. Suddenly, he was sucking it hard and she moaned in pleasure. He reached up and rubbed her clit as he sucked her asshole. She moaned and lifted her hips.

Suddenly, he stopped and stood up. He slipped off his pants, pulled off her thong and mounted her, plunging his dick deep into her cunt. She gasped as he entered her. His long, thick penis filled her up and pressed hard into the back of her vagina. It hurt slightly but the pressure was very erotic. Instead of moving in and out, he continued to press into her as he sucked her tongue and her lips, and as he thrust his tongue into her mouth.

After a few minutes, he began moving in and out. She was beside herself with pleasure. She wrapped her legs around him and she pulled her skirt up so it was not in the way. Then his movement became harder and stronger and she exploded with a powerful orgasm. She began to sob from the intensity of the feeling.

He waited until her reaction subsided and he pulled out and crouched over her face. "Suck it," he said. She took his dick into her mouth and she tasted her salty sweet cum. His dick was covered in her juice and she had a hard time taking even half of it into her mouth.

When he saw she was choking, he pulled out and began to masturbate over her. She couldn't believe she was actually seeing what she had been watching for so many months. Open your mouth, he said, and just as she did, he came. Her mouth filled up as huge squirts of cum spilled out of her mouth and down her cheeks.

He knelt beside her and put his tongue in her mouth. They shared his cum until they both had swallowed it. He licked her lips and her cheeks and then lay down beside her.

They watched the fire laying side by side. After a while, he unzipped her skirt and removed it. Then he lifted her top over her head and unsnapped her bra. He removed his shirt and leaned over her breasts and sucked her nipples. Soon, he was hard again. He reached between her legs and felt the wet. He spread her legs and entered her, moving slowly. She began to moan and he said, "Turn over." He placed her in a kneeling position and began to lick her ass again. Then he spit onto his dick and began to press into her anus.

"It hurts," she said, but he didn't back off. He kept pushing into her asshole as she cried in pain. His dick was so thick that he almost couldn't move it inside of her. Finally, he was completely in but it was difficult to move it in and out. Finally, he gave up and pulled it out. He flipped her over and entered her cunt again, and began pounding her hard and fast. "Harder," she said, "harder." They were both sweating from the exertion but they moved together in a frenzy. Suddenly she cried out and he let himself go. They came together in an explosion of cum.

Finally, he collapsed beside her and they fell asleep in front of the fire, sticky, wet and completely satisfied.

8.
The Sex Therapist

She had been seeing the sex therapist for six weeks now and the weekly sessions had consisted of talking about why she couldn't have an orgasm. It wasn't that she didn't like sex. In fact, she loved every aspect of lovemaking but no matter what her lovers did, she could not come.

She loved being touched in every way, having every orifice in her body penetrated, but she could only achieve an orgasm by herself, with a vibrator or two, so she knew she was missing something with her various lovers. Still, vibrators and other sex toys left her physically satisfied but emotionally unfulfilled.

As she headed down the street to the therapist's office, she became apprehensive. Today's session would involve something new. Today she would work with a surrogate. She didn't know what to expect but her therapist assured her she would be guided through the experience and that he would make sure she was comfortable in every way.

The therapist buzzed her into his brownstone office. He took her coat and asked her to sit on the sofa across from him. "We will take it very slowly," he told her. "Anytime you want to stop just say so. There's no need to worry."

He escorted her to the next room, a room she had never seen before. It was decorated like a spa with a massage table at the center, low lights, candles and dark drapes over the windows. The therapist pointed to a door and said, "That's the changing room. Please go in and remove your clothes and put on the robe you'll find on the hook and come out when you're ready."

She slowly peeled off her clothes having worn as little as possible so undressing would not be complicated. The soft terry cloth robe on the door was too large but heavy and warm and provided her some comfort. She paused before opening the door, trying to ease the knot in her stomach.

When she emerged, the therapist was sitting on a chair waiting for her. "I'll turn around while you get on the table. Remove the robe and get under the cover lying face down. Let me know when you're ready."

She slipped off the robe and slid under the cover. The table was warm and soft against her body and she pulled the flannel cover over herself. "I'm ready," she said.

"I want you to put on these eye shades," said the therapist. "I don't want you to be distracted by anything visual," he said. "I want you to focus only on what you feel. I will leave the room and your surrogate will be in momentarily."

Once he left the room, soft, calming music like she had heard before in spas began to play. She heard the door open and then softly close. Soft footsteps that sounded like moccasin-covered feet approached the massage table.

The moccasin wearer said nothing. He (she assumed it was a man) folded the blanket down to her waist and began to massage her neck, back and arms with warm, aromatic oil. She soon drifted into a relaxed, dreamy state. He covered her back and lifted the blanket off her legs. He began massaging her feet, then her calves and then her thighs. As he reached the top of her thighs he slid his hands under the blanket and began caressing her buttocks. She was so relaxed that she didn't flinch at the intimacy. Slowly, his hand slid between her legs. He gently massaged her lips and she began to become aroused. Soon she was wet and as she became increasingly more moist, he slid a finger, then two into her vagina.

Never before had she felt aroused like this. Lovemaking was generally urgent and erotic. Rarely did her lovers take the time to lull her into such a state of relaxation. In fact, her own urgency usually contributed to things moving faster than she liked.

She began raising herself to the therapist's fingers. Suddenly, he spoke, "Turn over," he said in a deep, smooth voice. She thought his voice alone could make her come.

She turned over and didn't care that the blanket slid away. He gently ran his hands over her stomach and her breasts, and then slid down to her vagina again. He spread her legs slightly and lifted her knees. Suddenly, she could feel the warm tip of a vibrator against her vagina. He rubbed it on the outside pressing down toward her anus. He did not let it go in but kept rubbing her on the outside, pressing slightly harder each time it reached her anus.

She became increasingly wet and began lifting herself toward the device. Still, he didn't put it in. She began to moan softly, lost in the darkness and the feel of the vibrator. Then she felt warm oil being dripped between her legs. It ran down to her anus and the therapist gently lifted her butt and slid a small foam wedge underneath. Suddenly, another vibrator was pressing against her ass. He pushed then retreated. Each time, he pushed a little harder and she responded to the pain with a grunt. It was larger than anything she had ever taken before.

Each time he pressed into her, he would retreat for a while to let the pain subside. Then he said to her, "When I say push, I want you to bear down. And when I tell you to relax, I want you to let your muscles go loose."

Suddenly, he turned the vibrator against her cunt on vibrate, but still, he did not let it go in. "Push," he said as he forced the other vibrator into her ass. It hurt her but felt strangely erotic. "Relax," he said as he pulled it out. "Push," he said a minute later. This time, it went further in. She moaned at the pain but the vibration on her cunt kept her aroused and offset the pain in her ass. He repeated this three more times and the last time, he slid the vibrator almost entirely into her ass. Now he reached for her hand and put it on her clitoris. Guiding her hand, he began instructing her to rub it back and forth, side to side, then up and down. Once she began following his lead, he opened her legs wider and slowly slid the first vibrator into her cunt.

Now, she was moaning and lost in the sensations that she felt inside of her. He pressed the vibrator up towards her stomach, not with an in-and-out motion, but just pressing into a spot that made her see lights behind her closed eyes.

He began gently moving the vibrator in her cunt, in the shortest arc possible. When the vibrator in her ass began to slide out he pushed it in as deep as it would go and held it there. Now both vibrators were pressing against her without movement. The only movement was her own hand on her clit.

Suddenly, she began to feel a familiar rising sensation like the one she was able to achieve when she masturbated herself. But this sensation was bigger and more explosive than anything she had felt before. Suddenly, it erupted and she couldn't stop herself from screaming. It lasted for what seemed like hours but only minutes had passed. When she quieted, the therapist removed the vibrators, one by one, and then wiped her with a warm wet cloth. He pressed her legs down and closed, and covered her with a warm blanket.

"Rest as long as you need to," he said. "Then you can get dressed." She heard his footsteps move towards the door, then the door opening and closing. She lay there for another ten minutes, relishing the residual feeling she had from the orgasm. She was sore but more satisfied than she had ever been before.

She got up slowly and slipped on the robe. She felt as if she could hardly walk. Back in the dressing room, she put on her clothes. She combed her hair and pulled herself together. She took a deep breath and opened the door.

Her therapist was waiting for her. She glanced over and saw that the wet covering on the massage table had been removed. She felt slightly embarrassed. "I believe we have had success," he said. She blushed and nodded.

"And now that we know what works for you, the next time you will practice with the surrogate. That way, when you make love, you will be able to show your lover how to make you come. A few more sessions, and you should be able to direct your lovemaking in a way that brings you satisfaction. I encourage you to practice between sessions and see if you can achieve the same result. I'll see you next week and we'll continue."

She nodded and he escorted her out of the office, Now, the only thing she wanted was to sleep.

9.
The Sex Club

He met her at a neighbor's party. She was sexy and flirtatious and they had had sex in his car. She had great tits, gave a good blow job and had a juicy cunt. Although he was not interested in her romantically, he enjoyed having sex with her periodically. Best yet, she was not demanding and did not seem to want a relationship.

For the past year, he had been a member of a sex club. Its membership rules were that there had to be an equal number of men and women, and they only invited a new member when someone dropped out. He had lost interest in it recently, but when his friend John told him they were looking for an additional woman, he thought about his periodic sex partner.

Although she seemed to be pretty open about sex, he wasn't sure how she would feel about a club. He called her and asked to come by. His visit went the usual way. He grabbed her as soon as he walked in the door and began kissing her passionately, sliding his hand into her pants making her immediately become wet.

She took his hand and led him to the bedroom. She slowly undressed him and they spent the next two hours fucking. After they had both come, he brought up the subject of the sex club.

"Listen," he said. "I want to tell you about something you might be interested in. There's this sex club and they're looking for a new member. They always have an even number of men and women and right now, they are down one woman. Do you think you'd be interested?"

"What kind of a sex club?" she asked. "Do they just get together and have orgies?"

"Well, it's more like parties where anything goes," he explained. "Sometimes it's one on one, sometimes two on one, even girl on girl. Sometimes people just watch and jerk off."

She laughed. "You mean the men jerk off."

He laughed also. "Well, I've seen women jerk off with vibrators and dildos. That's a turn-on too."

"So what do you have to do to become a member?" she asked.

"Well," he said, "there's an annual fee . . . and there is an initiation."

"What kind of initiation?" she asked.

"Three members get to 'initiate' the new member, basically get to do anything they want while everyone else watches," he explained.

"Like, it's nothing dangerous?" she asked. "No cutting or choking or beating?"

"No, no," he said. "It's all sex, but if you agree to join, you have to go through the initiation. There is no backing out once it starts. And you are sworn to secrecy. There are no names given. Only one person knows anything about you; that would be me. And the way we ensure secrecy is to threaten to expose you publicly. That keeps everyone quiet. Are you in?"

"Well, tell me what the past initiations have been like," she asked. "It varies," he said. "Depends on the people. Depends whose turn it is. Depends if its men or women and what they like. Whatever it is, you go along. Then you're in and you get to do what you like to do with whomever you want to do it with."

"OK, I'm intrigued," she said. "I'll give it a try."

~ ~ ~

A week later, he took her to the sex club. They met at a building in a manufacturing district. It looked like an old factory, but when they entered, there was a lobby where people were sitting around chatting and having drinks. He introduced her to a few people and then led her to a room full of lockers and robes.

"Take everything off and put your stuff in a locker. You can set your own code to lock it up and put on one of these robes," he said. "I'll meet you in the main room after I change."

Women began entering the locker room and disrobing. She noticed that everyone had a good body; nice tits and asses, everyone firm and fit. Thank god I won't have to look at gross people, she thought.

She followed the other women into a large room beyond the lobby. The room was carpeted with low couches throughout that had no backs or arms. In the center of the room was a raised platform and three men with open robes were standing around it. Two of them were stroking their penises; the third one was already erect. All three were well endowed and good-looking.

Her friend came up to her and led her over to the platform. "Are you ready?" he asked.

Just then, the lights in the room were dimmed. Only a spotlight on the platform remained bright. Men and women wearing robes began filtering into the room and took their places on the couches.

"I'll see you when you're done," her friend said, and he drifted over to a group of people at the side of the room.

One of the three men came up to her and slid off her robe. "Lay down on your stomach," he said. A triangular piece of foam was on the platform, and he guided her so that her ass was raised in the air. He put a small pillow under her head and then he slid her wrists into velvet straps at the edge of the platform that she hadn't noticed before. He tightened them before she could say anything and suddenly she began to panic.

"Relax," said the second man. "I promise we won't hurt you. You'll like it."

The first man began to finger her closed pussy while the second man rubbed oil on her ass. The third man continued to stroke his dick close to her face. His hard dick was smooth and pink. It had a large head that was already leaking cum. He leaned into her and said, "Open your mouth."

She began to suck his penis while the first man continued to stroke her pussy, with one finger then two. He then knelt down and looked at her smooth silky cunt lips. Her clit was hard and deep red and he leaned into her and sucked it. Her juices covered his face and she smelled of sweet cunt perfume. She was wet and aroused. She moaned and lifted her ass so the man could get his tongue deeper into her cunt.

She looked around. She could not see behind her but at the sides of the room, she could see men masturbating, others eating pussy. Each dick she could see was longer than the next one. She couldn't believe she was seeing so much dick at one time.

Suddenly she felt something in her ass. "Tonight you are going to take the 'egg' said the first man. What she couldn't see was a vibrator that was a normal size at each end, but the middle was the shape of a large egg."

The man slid the slender end into her ass and she moaned with pleasure. She loved anal intercourse. He slid it in and out several times until he got to the round end of the egg. "When I tell you to push," he said, "push hard! And when I tell you to relax, relax your muscles. It will be easier if you listen to me and do it when I tell you."

Suddenly he said, "Push" and she felt a searing pain. "Oh my god," she cried. "You're hurting me!"

"Relax," he said and he pulled the vibrator out and slid a smooth rounded shaft of ice into her ass. "Relax," he said again. After a minute, he put the vibrator back in her ass and told her to push. "Push harder," he said as he forced the egg halfway into her ass.

Her ass was now wide open and she cried, "Please take it out. It hurts."

"OK, I'll back off," he said, "but you'll have to help me get it out. Relax now so I can ease it out," but he held it where it was. "OK, now push it out. Help me get it out. Push, push harder than before and it will come out."

She grunted as she pushed and he eased the egg out a bit and said, "Push, push just a little bit more. It's coming," he said. "One more push and it will be out." Just as she pushed harder, he pushed the vibrator deeper into her ass until the egg suddenly disappeared inside her. She moaned in pain. Only the other narrow end of the vibrator could be seen in her ass.

She was whimpering and sweating and he put an icy cold compress on her asshole.

"OK, the worst is over now," he said.

"Who's going first," asked the first man.

"I called it," said the second man. He pushed a button on the vibrator in her ass and it began to vibrate in a pulsing motion. He leaned over her and slipped his dick into her cunt. He could feel the vibrator in her ass that made her cunt feel tight. He fucked her for about five minutes as she lifted her ass up to him in rhythm with his movements. Then he came on her ass making a deep sighing sound of relief. "I didn't want to mess her up for the next guy," he said to the men next to him.

The third man who had been fucking her mouth earlier, leaned over and saw that her cunt was stretched open so that he could see the flesh inside. He began fucking her and he pushed down on her ass to feel the vibrator even more on his dick. It took only a few thrusts before he came inside her. "Sorry," he said to the first man. "I couldn't help it."

"That's ok," said the first man. "I have another idea." He rubbed the woman's ass around the vibrator with lubricant. With his finger, he rubbed the lube inside alongside the vibrator. Then he slowly forced his dick into her ass alongside the vibrator. She moaned. Once he was in, he leaned over and slid his hands onto her tits. "My god, you feel good," he said. "You want it, don't you?"

He had never felt anything so tight before. The feeling of her tight ass, the pulsing of the vibrator, the feel of her tits in his hands made him explode in her ass. As soon as he came, he slipped out. The three men stood there looking exhausted.

The woman was sweaty and sticky with cum all over her ass, her back and her cunt. Another man came over and said, "I'll take care of her."

"Listen babe," he said. "Let's get this thing out of you. Just relax and I'll pull it out." It came out easily because she was so stretched out. Once he removed it, her asshole looked huge. He untied her hands and led her to the showers. "You did great," he said. "There were lots of orgasms here tonight watching you get fucked. From now on, you'll have the enjoyment of watching others."

In the shower, she looked exhausted and shaky. He got into the shower with her and soaped her up, rubbing her breasts, between her legs and around her ass. She began rubbing his dick with the soap and in just a few minutes, he came. They both rinsed off and dried one another. The man handed her a clean robe. He led her back into the main room and when she entered, people applauded and whistled.

"That was really hot," one woman said to her. "You have a gorgeous ass and cunt." The man next to her said, "Yeah, look at my dick. I've got enough of a hard on to fuck three women and with that he bent over the woman next to him and began to fuck her. Some people in the room were lying around exhausted from coming. Others were giving and getting blow jobs. One woman was sliding up and down another man's dick as she sat on his lap with her back to him.

The room smelled of cum. I'm going to like this, she thought. And she did.

61

10.

Girl on Girl

Their dorm rooms were across the hall from one another. Molly was shy and hadn't dated much although she was not a virgin. She was petite and slender with small breasts, a pretty face, short brown hair and a pale complexion.

Chris was taller and had an athletic build with muscular shoulders and narrow hips. She had a Mick Jagger kind of look about her and was always tanned. She knew everyone thought she was cool and she walked with great confidence.

It wasn't likely that Chris would befriend Molly, but she did, and Molly was flattered that Chris would take an interest in her. They hung out in one another's rooms, ate together at the college hangout in town, and went shopping for clothes in Chris's favorite shops. Molly knew that Chris dated one of the football players, and on weekends, her friend would disappear, spending time at her boyfriend's apartment.

One day during the week, Chris invited Molly to go with her to her boyfriend's apartment. "He's not home now," she said. "Let's just hang out there for a while." After they got there, Chris showed Molly around and they snagged two bottles of beer from the fridge. "Let me show you something," said Chris and they plopped down on the couch close together. Chris opened a drawer in the coffee table and pulled out a pile of photos. There were some of Chris in lace lingerie, some with Chris's boyfriend with his hands in her underwear, and others of him removing her underwear and of them naked together.

Molly was shocked but didn't want her friend to think that she was uncool, so she looked at them nonchalantly. "Do these turn you on?" asked Chris. "A little," said Molly tentatively. Chris put her hand on Molly's thigh and rubbed it lightly. "I like getting turned on by pictures," said Chris. "And by porn too. Have you ever watched porn," asked Chris. "No," said Molly and before Molly could object, Chris grabbed her boyfriend's laptop and googled "sex videos." She clicked on the first site and then opened a free video showing a woman moving a large dildo in and out of another woman's cunt.

As Molly watched with fascination, Chris put her hands between Molly's legs and began rubbing her cunt through her jeans. At first Molly felt uncomfortable, but then she began to feel wet and turned on. But she was not sure how to react. She looked up to Chris so much that she didn't want to offend her, but she had never done anything more sexual that have sex with her high school boyfriend in the basement of his house. It had not been more than a few minutes in the missionary position before he came, and she had never experienced an orgasm.

Suddenly, Chris reached over and kissed her on the lips. She put her tongue into Molly's mouth and ran it over her lips. At first, Molly did not kiss back but within a few minutes, she was responding to Chris's kisses. Chris unbuttoned Molly's jeans and reached her hand in to finger Molly's cunt. Molly was surprised at how wet she had become and how good this felt. She had never felt this way with her old boyfriend.

Chris stood up and lifted her sweater over her head and stepped out of her jeans. She had no underwear on and Molly couldn't help but admire how beautiful Chris's body was. Her stomach was flat and hard, her breasts small but full, her legs and arms muscular, and her butt rock hard.

"Take off your clothes," Chris said to Molly. Molly stood up and un-zipped her jeans and Chris slid them down along with Molly's underwear. Before Molly could even step out of her pants, Chris was on her knees licking Molly's clit and pushing a finger into her vagina. Molly couldn't help but moan and she felt liquid running down her legs.

"Let's go into the bedroom," said Chris. She helped Molly step out of her jeans and she lifted off Molly's shirt. She put her lips to Molly's breast and began sucking her nipple. She then took Molly by the hand and led her to the bed. She lay Molly down on the bed and spread her legs wide. She knelt over her and inserted her tongue as deep as she could into Molly's cunt while she rubbed Molly's clit with her thumb.

Molly moaned softly. Chris reached over to the night table and pulled a vibrator out of the drawer. Molly watched as Chris slowly slid the vibrator into her cunt. It was much bigger than her boyfriend's cock and it reached deeper than her boyfriend ever had.

Chris removed the vibrator from Molly's cunt and put it in her mouth. "Mmm," she said. "You taste good." Then Chris lay down on the bed, spread her legs and put the vibrator in her cunt. "You do me," Chris said to Molly, and Molly reached over and began moving the vibrator in and out of her friend's cunt. "Kiss me," said Chris and Molly kissed her and for the first time, put her tongue in Chris's mouth.

"I have a better idea," said Chris after a few minutes, and she reached into the drawer and pulled out a long dildo with a cock head at either end. "Let's fuck each other at the same time," she said. They sat facing each other on the bed and Chris positioned the dildo so that each end was in the other's cunt. They scooted closer to one another so that the dildo was deeply inside each one of them. They moved back and forth toward one another. Suddenly, Molly began to moan. She felt a sensation coming over her that she had never felt before. She made an animal-like sound and then began to softly cry. It was her first orgasm and she was overwhelmed.

Just then, Chris and Molly heard the front door open. "Oh shit," said Chris. "Marcus is home." A tall, handsome young black man stood in the doorway of the bedroom. "What the fuck," he said as he saw the two women lying on the bed with the dildo still in each of them.

"Hi Baby," said Chris. "We were just having some fun." Molly pulled away from the dildo and jumped off the bed, trying to cover herself with her hands. "It's o.k.," Chris said to Molly. "We were just fucking around," she said to Marcus. "Why don't you come and join us?"

He stared at Molly who looked like a frightened waif. He felt sorry for her because he knew how Chris was and that she probably talked this girl into something. "It's o.k.," he said to Molly. "I'm not going to touch you. This bitch can talk anyone into anything."

"Baby," said Chris. "How can you talk like that? You're always telling me how you would like to do a three-way, so now here's your chance."

Chris slid the dildo out of her cunt and came over to Marcus. "Don't be mad baby," she said. "This is Molly. Remember I was telling you about how nice she is? She really is delicious and I bet she wouldn't mind playing with us, would you Molly?"

"She looks like a scared rabbit," said Marcus, "and I'm not fucking any scared white girl."

"I'm not scared," said Molly. She was surprised that the words even came out of her mouth.

"Come Molly," said Chris and she reached for Molly's hand and led her back to the bed. "Do you want to watch us baby?" Chris asked Marcus. Before he could respond, Chris positioned herself next to Molly to perform 69. Chris began licking Molly but Molly had never done this before and she was hesitant. First, she began exploring Chris's cunt, noticing how pink and plump her labia and clit were. Then she slowly began licking Chris's clit, and then became more aggressive and started sucking her clit, making it extend longer than it had been.

She was so involved in the sensation of sucking and being sucked that she didn't realize that Marcus had removed his clothes and lay down next to Chris on the bed. When he tried to slide his dick into Chris, he hit Molly in the face. At first, she recoiled but Marcus said, "Suck it," and she lamely licked his dick.

"Damn," he said to Chris. "This girl doesn't know how to suck dick. Show her how." Chris turned around and kneeled over Marcus and took the full length of him – all 8 inches of thick dick – into her mouth. She sucked him hard as she moved up and down over him. Marcus moaned and suddenly turned her over with her ass in the air and slid his dick into her cunt. He moved slowly at first and then more rapidly, Chris moaned and quickly came with a long, loud moan.

Marcus pulled out and let Chris lay down on the bed. He turned to Molly who sat wide-eyed watching the action. "Want some?" asked Marcus and before she could answer, he laid her down on her back and entered her missionary style. He was so much larger than her high school boyfriend. She couldn't believe how good it felt to have him fill her up. He moved in a slow steady rhythm for about 10 minutes. She held on to him and didn't want him to stop. She wrapped her legs around his waist and moved with him. Suddenly, he pulled out and came all over her stomach and her chest. He rolled off of her and pulled Chris to him. He wrapped his arms around her and pulled her to his chest. The two of them promptly fell asleep.

Molly got up and went to the bathroom. She found a washcloth and wiped herself off. This had been a very erotic experience, but now she felt alone and very excluded as Chris and Marcus lay wrapped together on the bed. She walked back to the living room and found her clothes on the floor. As she was putting them on, Marcus appeared in the doorway. "Hey, where are you going?" he asked. "I'm going back to the dorm," she said. "No, don't go," said Marcus. "Stay here tonight with us. Let's order a pizza and hang out."

~ ~ ~

Later that evening, the three of them lay on the bed watching TV and eating pizza. When the pizza was gone, Marcus reached over and started rubbing Molly's neck. He leaned over and kissed her and she kissed him back. Chris began masturbating Marcus until he was completely hard. Marcus sat up and turned Molly around so she was on her knees and her ass was in the air. He pulled her cheeks apart and stuck his tongue into her asshole. She was shocked that someone could do this and she tightened up. "Relax," he said and he pulled her cheeks apart more. He covered his finger with saliva and slid a finger into her ass.

Chris slid around to face Molly and she began kissing her. Now Marcus positioned his dick to enter Molly's ass. As he began, she tried to pull away, but Marcus held onto her hips and would not allow her to retreat. Chris held her face and kissed her so that she couldn't speak. Marcus slowly pressed his dick into Molly's ass and she began to whimper against Chris's mouth. Finally, Marcus' dick was entirely inside Molly and he spit on his dick as it came out to lubricate the action. After he fucked Molly's ass for a few minutes, he pulled out and pulled Chris toward him. He positioned her standing and bent over the side of the bed. He lubed her ass and began fucking her harder than he fucked Molly. Chris reached down and rapidly manipulated her clit. "That's it baby," he said, "make yourself come."

Chris let out a howl as she came and then Marcus exploded inside her. They stood there after coming and when Marcus pulled out, cum dripped out of her ass. Marcus knelt over and licked her ass. Molly couldn't believe what she saw. She had no idea that sex could be this raunchy. She was repulsed and fascinated at the same time.

"Let's go take a shower," said Marcus and he led the two girls into the bathroom. They soaped one another, rinsed and helped each other towel off. All three were worn out from fucking and coming. They lie down in the bed and promptly fell asleep. The morning would bring another round of sex, and this time, Molly would be as eager a participant as Chris and Marcus. The night of sex would be one of only many they would spend together, but for now, they slept.